FANTASY
FABLES

BEDTIME STORIES FOR
YOUNG MINDS AND HEARTS

FANTASY FABLES

JENNIFER MIDDLETON

LTDF Publishing
WEST CHESTER, PENNSYLVANIA

LDTF Publishing
1525 Brian Drive
West Chester, PA 19380

Publisher's Note: This is a work of fiction. Names, characters, places, and incidents are a product of the author's imagination. Locales and public names are sometimes used for atmospheric purposes. Any resemblance to actual people, living or dead, or to businesses, companies, events, institutions, or locales is completely coincidental.

Book Layout ©2023 LTDF Publishing

Ordering Information:
Quantity sales. Special discounts are available on quantity purchases by corporations, associations, and others. For details, contact the "Special Sales Department" at the address above.

Fantasy Fables – Bedtime Stories for Young Minds and Hearts/Jennifer Middleton. — 1st ed.
ISBN 979-8-218-15358-8

To my loving husband, who has been my rock, support, and inspiration source. Your unwavering love and encouragement have been invaluable throughout this journey, and I am forever grateful for your presence in my life. This book is a testament to our beautiful and unbreakable bond, and I am proud to dedicate it to you with heartfelt appreciation. I love you now and always.

And to my two precious children, my little boy and girl. You bring so much joy and wonder into my life, and I am endlessly proud of the imaginative and creative individuals you are growing up to be. Your endless curiosity and love for stories inspire me every day, and I am thankful for the laughter and love we share. With all my love, I dedicate this book to you, my little storytellers.

"Every child should have a library of books they love and cherish, a place to escape to and dream, a place to feel safe and secure."

—JACQUELINE WILSON

A WORD FOR THE READER

*A*S A PARENT or somebody who cares for a child, you have a unique and powerful opportunity to shape your child's imagination, beliefs, and values through the stories you share with them. That's why I've carefully crafted this collection of short stories to not only entertain but also educate, and inspire your child.

Each story is set in today's society and infused with a touch of fantasy and whimsy, making them perfect for 4 to 8-year-olds. These stories are designed to promote good character and show the consequences of poor choices, demonstrating the importance of making the right decisions.

These stories are not just ordinary tales, they are thought-provoking and encourage children to reflect on the world around them. From themes of bravery, determination, and kindness to exploring inner and outer beauty, each story is designed to spark meaningful conversations and encourage critical thinking.

Additionally, it's essential to understand that some stories may include conflicts, battles, and confrontations between characters. However, there are no graphic depictions of violence or explicit imagery. Children will have to use their imagination and previous experiences to fill in the missing pieces of the story, making it a more engaging and personalized experience. It is always a good idea for parents to preview a story before sharing it with their child, so they can assess the content and make an informed decision on what is best for their child's development and interests.

To further reinforce the principle of the story, make sure to talk to your child about it after reading. Engage in a conversation and ask them what they thought of the story, what they learned, and how they can apply what they learned to their own lives. Some Fun and Serious questions are at the end of each chapter to get the conversation going.

It's also essential to follow up with your child after a week or two to reinforce the principle of the story and help them internalize the lesson. This will ensure they remember the story and its message for years, making it a valuable and lasting learning experience.

Storytelling plays a vital role in a child's development, and I hope this collection will provide a fun and educational experience for you and your child. So, settle in and get ready for an imaginative and thought-provoking journey through the pages of this book.

ONE

The Power of the Heart: The Story of Ella and Shadow

In tonight's story, you will follow a brave girl named Ella as she goes on a magical adventure to defeat an evil creature and show the importance of being kind to others.

⌁

ONCE UPON A time, in a magical kingdom where humans, animals, and mythical creatures coexisted, there lived a young girl named Ella. She was adventurous and curious, always eager to explore and help others.

One day, while Ella was exploring the forest, she heard rumors of a mysterious creature named Shadow who had appeared and begun to terrorize the kingdom. Shadow was selfish and cruel, caring only for himself and showing no empathy towards others. The kingdom was filled with fear, and Ella knew she had to do something to restore peace.

So, she set out on a journey to defeat Shadow. Ella encountered many obstacles, but her kindness and compassion never wavered. She helped a lost unicorn find its way back to its herd, tended to a frightened bird with a broken wing, and even aided a group of lost bunnies who were afraid to return to their warren. Ella earned the trust and gratitude of those she met everywhere she went.

It took a while for Ella to make her way through the forest, but she finally arrived at Shadow's lair. She took a deep breath and stepped forward to face him.

"Who are you?" Shadow growled.

"I am Ella," she said as she stiffened her back and raised her head. "I am here to stop you."

Shadow laughed. "You? Stop me?" Shadow moved closer to Ella. "You're just a little girl. You're no match for me."

Ella stood her ground. "I may be just a little girl, but I have something much more powerful than physical strength." Ella placed her hand over her heart. "I have kindness in my heart; that is the greatest power of all."

Shadow stumbled backward. His mind raced and his dark eyes shifted back and forth. Was this little girl right?

"No," Shadow said at the top of his deep voice. "Being cruel is more powerful than your kindness."

Shadow leaped at Ella and they clashed in a fierce battle. Despite the odds against her, Ella's kindness and compassion proved too much for Shadow, and he was forced to retreat.

With peace restored to the kingdom, Ella returned home as a hero. From that day on, she was the bravest and kindest girl in the kingdom.

Ella continued to explore and help others, always spreading kindness and compassion wherever she went, and the kingdom lived happily ever after, with Ella as a shining example of the power of a kind and courageous heart.

⋘

For the reader:

This story, *The Power of the Heart*, highlights the importance of kindness and compassion. The character of Ella shows that even a young child can make a difference in the world through her actions. Ella's journey teaches children that they have the power to overcome challenges and defeat evil thoughts through kindness and compassion. The story also emphasizes that inner strength and a kind heart are more powerful than physical strength and that these qualities can bring about positive change in the world. This story is a valuable lesson for children about the importance of being kind and compassionate and their power to make a difference in the world.

Fun questions about the story:

- What kind of journey did Ella go on in the story?
- What did Ella do to defeat Shadow?

Serious questions about the principles:

- What kind of power does Ella possess that helps her in her mission?
- How do Ella's kindness and compassion help her win the battle against Shadow?

TWO

The Heart of Giving: A Fairy's Journey

In tonight's story, we will learn about the joy of giving and how it can bring happiness to both the giver and the receiver in a magical kingdom filled with talking animals and enchanted forests.

⚜

ONCE UPON A time, a young fairy named Amber lived in a magical kingdom filled with talking animals and enchanted forests. She was always on the lookout for adventure and loved to spread joy wherever she went.

One day, Amber set off on a journey to find the true joy of giving. She flew through the kingdom, meeting all sorts of creatures and asking them about their experiences with giving.

Amber stopped to chat with a rabbit who was munching on some carrots.

"Excuse me, dear rabbit," she said. "Have you ever experienced the joy of giving?"

"I have," the rabbit said. "But I don't think it's as important as keeping my carrots safe."

Amber fluttered away and flew down the trail, where she came across a grumpy old dragon named Greed. Greed hoarded all the treasure in the kingdom and refused to give up any of it.

"Greetings, Greed," said Amber. "Can you tell me about the joy of giving?"

"Joy of giving?" growled Greed. "Nonsense! Hoarding is the only way to keep what's yours."

Amber stood before Greed, her eyes shining with hope. She lifted her arms and gestured to the world around them.

"Look at all the creatures here in our kingdom," Amber said. "Each time one of them shares a treasure or a kind word, do you not see the happiness it brings?"

Greed crossed his arms and scrunched his forehead. "I see the happiness it brings to the receiver," he grumbled. "But I don't believe it brings happiness to the giver."

Amber smiled, a gentle expression spreading across her face.

"You don't have to take my word for it," she said. "Come, join me on a journey. Let's observe the joy of giving together and see the happiness it brings to both the giver and the receiver."

Greed was hesitant at first, but Amber's kindness and determination won him over. Together, they set out on a journey through the kingdom, observing all the acts of giving they encountered along the way.

As they traveled, they saw a squirrel sharing nuts with a bird. They watched as a deer gave its antlers to a younger deer in need. And they saw the smiles and laughter of the givers each time they saw the happiness their giving brought to the receivers.

By the end of their journey, Greed was no longer skeptical. He saw the truth in Amber's words and felt the joy of giving for himself.

"I understand now," Greed said, a smile spreading across his face. "Giving truly does bring happiness to both the giver and the receiver."

Amber beamed, proud of her friend and the lesson he had learned. And from that day on, the kingdom was filled with even more acts of kindness and joy, all thanks to Amber's unwavering belief in the power of giving.

And so, Greed gave away all of his treasure, and the kingdom was filled with happiness and light.

Amber learned a valuable lesson on her journey: that the joy of giving is something that all can experience. And from that day on, she lived her life spreading the message of giving and the joy it brings, touching the hearts of all she encountered along the way.

❧

For the reader:

This story, *The Heart of Giving,* is a valuable lesson for parents and children about giving. The story shows how giving can bring joy and happiness, not just to the recipient but to the giver as well. The story demonstrates that hoarding material possessions only leads to loneliness and unhappiness, whereas giving freely and with a kind heart can lead to lasting joy and friendship. The story encourages children to embrace the joy of giving and experience its positive impact on their own lives and those around them.

Fun questions about the story:

- What was Amber's quest in the story, and why did she go on this adventure?
- How did Greed react when Amber tried to teach him about the joy of giving? Can you give an example of what he said or did?

Serious questions about the principles:

- How did Amber's journey help her understand the joy of giving?
- How do you think the kingdom would have been different if Greed continued to hoard all the treasure?

THREE

Defeating Malice: The Story of Timmy and the Witch

In tonight's story, we learn about a young boy named Timmy who sets out to save his village from a witch and discovers the importance of being brave and helping others.

❧

ONCE UPON A time, in a magical world filled with creatures and strange powers, there was a small village known for its peace and prosperity. But there was always a dark shadow lurking around, waiting to cast its fear upon the villagers. The villagers lived in constant fear of the evil witch, Malice.

Timmy was just seven years old and lived in the village. One day, he was playing outside when he noticed something strange happening in the village. People were disappearing, and no one knew why.

"What's going on?" Timmy said his friend Sarah.

"Everyone's afraid," Sarah said. "They say the witch, Malice, is behind it."

Timmy's heart sank. He knew the witch was a cruel and selfish woman who loved spreading fear and terror. But he was brave, kind, and always eager to help others. He dreamed of becoming a great hero one day and saving the world. He was determined to stop the witch and save the villagers.

"I'm going to find out what's going on," Timmy said. "I'll stop the witch and save the villagers."

Sarah looked at Timmy with a soft smile and worried eyes. "Be careful," she said. "The witch is powerful and won't give up without a fight."

Timmy set out on his journey, determined to find the witch, and stop her. He traveled through the magical world, braving dangerous creatures and using his quick thinking to solve puzzles and overcome obstacles. He met magical creatures along the way who taught him about bravery, kindness, and the power of friendship.

Along the way, Timmy came across a wise old wizard who told him about the witch's castle and warned him of the dangers he would face.

"The witch is powerful, young one," the wizard said. "She will stop at nothing to defeat you. You must be brave and never give up."

Timmy thanked the wizard for his advice and continued on his journey. He finally reached the witch's castle, and as he approached the front gates, he could feel his heart beating faster and faster. He was scared, but he refused to give up. He remembered why he had started his journey in the first place and found the courage to stand up to the witch.

As he entered the castle, the witch appeared before him, and she was more frightening than Timmy could have ever imagined.

"You're a brave little boy," the witch said with a sinister smile. "But you're no match for me. I have all the power, and you have nothing."

Timmy was terrified, but he refused to back down. "I may not have your power," Timmy said, "but I have something even stronger - my bravery and my desire to help others." Timmy stepped towards the witch. "That's why I came here, to stop you and save the villagers."

The witch laughed and raised her wand high in the air. She cast a spell to capture Timmy.

But Timmy was quick and nimble, and he was able to dodge the spell. He used his bravery and quick thinking to outsmart the witch, breaking her spell and defeating her in a magical duel.

With the witch defeated, Timmy returned to the village as a hero. The villagers cheered and celebrated, grateful for his bravery and determination. Timmy had shown them that even a young boy could make a difference and help others, and he had inspired them to be brave and face their fears.

And from that day forward, the village was again filled with peace and prosperity, and Timmy was known as the bravest little hero in all the land.

∽

For the reader:

This story, *Defeating Malice,* demonstrates the importance of bravery, determination, and kindness. It shows that even a young child like Timmy can make a difference and help others. Timmy's bravery and quick thinking, combined with his desire to help others, allowed him to defeat the evil witch and save the village. This story inspires children to be brave, face their fears, and never give up on adversity. It also teaches the value of friendship and the power of kindness, demonstrating that even a small act of bravery can have a big impact on the world.

Fun questions about the story:

- What was Timmy's plan to stop the witch and save the village?
- What did Timmy learn about bravery and helping others in the story?

Serious questions about the principles:

- What is an essential lesson Timmy learned in the story about being brave and helping others?
- How would you have acted if you were in Timmy's shoes, facing the witch and trying to save the villagers? What would you do to be brave and help others in a similar situation?

FOUR

The Power of Patience: Ava's Quest to Save the Magical World

In tonight's story, we follow Ava as she learns about the importance of waiting for the right time and how being patient can lead to amazing things.

ONCE UPON A time, in a magical world filled with enchanted forests, talking animals, and whimsical creatures, lived a 10-year-old girl named Ava. She was curious, adventurous, and always eager to explore her world. But she had a problem, Ava was impatient. She wanted everything to happen right now and didn't like to wait.

One day, as Ava was exploring the enchanted forest, she met a talking rabbit.

"Why are you in such a hurry?" the rabbit said.

"I just am," Ava said with a quick huff. "I don't like to wait." Ava stared down at the rabbit and tilted her head.

"Well, you might want to slow down," the rabbit said as he thumped his foot. "There's a wicked witch named Morgath and she's jealous of your magical world." Thump, thump went the rabbit's foot. "She's determined to stop you from discovering the true power of patience."

Ava's heart raced and her skin tingled. This was not what she expected. "What can I do to stop her?"

"You must learn the value of patience," the rabbit said. "Morgath will create challenges for you. Thump, thump. "But you must face them with a calm and patient heart. Only then will you be able to protect your magical world." The rabbit turned and hopped into the woods.

With determination in her heart, Ava set out on her journey to learn the value of patience. Along the way, she encountered obstacles, but she remained calm and patient, knowing that the fate of her world depended on her ability to wait.

As Ava walked, she heard a wise old owl calling out to her, "Why are you so patient?"

"I'm learning that good things come to those who wait," Ava said with a smile.

"That's right," the owl said, "patience is a powerful gift. It allows you to see the world differently and gives you the strength to face any challenge."

Finally, Ava reached Morgath's lair. It was covered with spider webs and smelled of mold.

The wicked witch was waiting for her, and she was ready to do battle.

"You're too late!" Morgath cackled. "I've already taken control of your magical world."

Ava stood tall and replied, "I may be late, but I'm not defeated." Thump, thump beat Ava's heart. She took in a long breath. "I have the gift of patience, which gives me the strength to face you."

With a calm and patient heart, Ava defeated Morgath and restored peace to her magical world. From that day forward, Ava learned that the true power of patience was not in rushing through life, but in taking the time to enjoy each moment and appreciate the world around her.

From that day on, Ava no longer rushed through her days. She savored each moment, taking in the beauty of her world. The talking animals and whimsical creatures were amazed at how patient Ava had become, and they all lived happily ever after in peace and harmony.

∽

For the reader:

The story, *The Gift of Patience*, showcases the importance of slowing down and thinking about things, a valuable life lesson for children. By following the journey of Ava, the young protagonist who learns to overcome her impatience, the story demonstrates the positive outcomes that can result from waiting and being patient. Through the challenges posed by the wicked witch, Morgath, Ava learns the power of patience and how it can protect her magical world. This story teaches children that good things come to those who wait, and that patience is the key to unlocking their full potential. By instilling these values in children, the story can help them develop resilience and perseverance and better understand the world around them.

Fun questions about the story:

- What was Ava's magical world like, and what kind of creatures did she encounter?
- What did Ava learn about patience, and why do you think it's important?

Serious questions about the story:

- What is the most important lesson Ava learned in the story?
- How can being patient help us in our own lives?

FIVE

Forgiveness and the Sorcerer's Curse

In tonight's story, "The Magic of Forgiveness", we follow a brave girl named Emily as she goes on an adventure to save the kingdom and learns about the power of forgiveness in relationships.

≪

ONCE UPON A time, in a magical world filled with enchanted forests, talking animals, and magical creatures, there lived a 10-year-old girl named Emily. She was well known in her village for her kindness, caring nature, and willingness to help others.

Emily was always curious about the world around her and longed to explore it more. So, one day, she decided to go on an adventure. But she soon learned that the kingdom was in trouble. A wicked sorcerer named Grendel casts a spell of darkness over the land, causing all the creatures to stop caring and become sad. The kingdom was in desperate need of a hero to save it.

Emily huffed and blew her cheek out. "This has to stop," she said as she looked into the woods with squinted eyes.

Emily bravely decided to set out on a quest to save the kingdom. She traveled through enchanted forests and across rolling hills, meeting all sorts of creatures along the way. Some creatures warned her of the dangers ahead, while others offered to help her on her journey.

One day, Emily met a talking squirrel who had a message for her. "Emily," the squirrel said, "you must forgive Grendel if you want to break the curse and save the kingdom."

"Forgive Grendel?" said Emily, her eyes opening wide. "How can I forgive someone who's done so much evil?"

"Forgiveness is a powerful thing," the squirrel said. "It can change the world." The little squirrel picked up a nut and stuffed it into its mouth. "When you forgive someone, it sets you free and opens the door to a brighter future."

Emily didn't understand how this could be possible, but she was determined to try. She continued her journey and finally came face to face with Grendel.

Grendel squinted her eyes and waved her arms over her head. She bit her lip and began to speak the spell as she curled her fingers.

"Grendel," said Emily, "I forgive you for all the evil you've done."

Grendel cackled. "Forgive me? You're just a little girl." She pointed at Emily. "What makes you think you can forgive me?"

"Forgiveness is a magical power," said Emily. "It can break the curse and restore the kingdom to happiness."

Grendel looked at Emily for a long time, then he sighed. "Very well," he said. "I forgive you too."

As soon as the words were spoken, the curse was broken. The kingdom was filled with light and life once again. All the creatures were restored to their former selves, and the kingdom was filled with happiness and joy.

Emily returned to her village as a hero. She had saved the kingdom and learned a valuable lesson about the power of forgiveness. From that day on, she lived happily ever after, and the kingdom was at peace for many years.

"Wow," said the squirrel as he looked around at the kingdom for another nut. "I think you just taught us all a valuable lesson about forgiveness. It is a powerful thing."

"It certainly is." Emily smiled. "And I'm so glad I could experience it for myself."

⇜

For the reader:

The story, Forgiveness and the Sorcerer's Curse, explores the principle that forgiveness is a crucial lesson for children as it helps foster healthy relationships with themselves and others. When a child learns to forgive, they can let go of negative feelings and resentment, leading to better communication, understanding, and trust. This, in turn, leads to stronger and more meaningful relationships where individuals can support and grow with one another. Additionally, forgiveness can lead to increased feelings of empathy, compassion, and kindness, which are essential traits for children to develop as they grow and navigate the world around them. By emphasizing the power of forgiveness, this story teaches children a valuable lesson they can carry with them throughout their lives.

Fun questions about the story:

- What do you think was the most important lesson Emily learned on her quest?
- Can you think of a time when you had to forgive someone, or when someone forgave you?

Serious questions about the story:

- What did you learn about forgiveness from the story of Emily and Grendel?
- How do you think forgiveness can help people in their relationships and everyday life?

SIX

Jack and the Shadow Monster: A Quest for Truth

In tonight's story, "The Strength of Honesty," you will follow a brave and truthful girl named Lily as she goes on an adventure to defeat a monster who spreads lies and deceit, and learn about the importance of always being honest.

⤵

ONCE UPON A time, a little boy named Jack lived in a magical world filled with fantastical creatures and enchanted forests. He lived in a small village surrounded by an enchanted forest and he was known for his curious, brave nature and honesty.

One day, a mysterious creature known as the Shadow Monster began to spread lies and deceit throughout the village. Chaos and confusion reigned as the villagers struggled to distinguish truth from fiction.

Determined to end the Shadow Monster's reign of terror, Jack set out on a quest to find the source of its power and defeat it once and for all. With the help of his friends, Peter and Lucy, he entered the enchanted forest, determined to find the monster and bring an end to its lies.

As they journeyed deeper into the forest, Jack and his friends came across a talking tree.

"Beware, young travelers!" said Talking Tree as it waved it branches in the air. "The Shadow Monster ahead is not to be trifled with. It spreads lies and deceit wherever it goes, leaving only chaos and confusion in its wake."

"Don't worry, we're not afraid," Jack said as he puffed out his chest. "We're on a quest to defeat the Shadow Monster and restore truth to the land."

The Talking Tree smiled. "Well then, let me tell you a secret." The branches of the Talking Tree stopped. "The Shadow Monster's greatest weakness is the truth." A long branch waved Jack closer. "If you can hold onto it and never let go, you will be able to defeat it."

Encouraged by the talking tree's words, Jack and his friends continued their quest, determined to find the Shadow Monster and end its lies.

As they drew closer, they could see the Shadow Monster's dark and ominous figure shrouded in shadows.

"Ha! So you think you can defeat me, do you?" said the

Shadow Monster. "I have been spreading lies and deceit for centuries, and no one has ever been able to stop me."

"We may not be able to stop you," Jack said, "but we can certainly expose you for what you are."

"Pah!" the Shadow Monster said with sneered lips. "Truth is nothing but a weak and feeble concept. It is the lies that have given me my power, and it is the lies that will keep me in control."

"Not if I have anything to say about it," Jack stepped closer. "The truth is always stronger in the end, and I will make sure that everyone knows the truth about you."

Jack and his friends launched into battle against the Shadow Monster. Despite its attempts to spread more lies and confusion, they were determined to defeat it and restore truth to the land.

The battle was fierce, with the Shadow Monster using every trick in its arsenal to try and defeat Jack and his friends. But Jack held onto the truth, never letting go, and slowly but surely, the Shadow Monster's power began to weaken.

Finally, with a final burst of energy, Jack delivered the last blow, defeating the Shadow Monster once and for all. Its power over the land was forever shattered, and truth and honesty were restored.

Jack and his friends returned to the village, where they were hailed as heroes. From that day forward, Jack was known as the boy who brought truth and honesty back to the land, and he lived a happy and fulfilled life surrounded by his friends and loved ones.

And the villagers learned that the greatest weapon against lies and deceit was the truth and that it was always worth fighting for, no matter what.

※

For the reader:

This story, *Jack and the Shadow Monster*, demonstrates the importance of honesty and truthfulness for children. Through Jack's journey to defeat the Shadow Monster and restore truth to her village, children will learn that honesty is always the best policy and that it has the power to overcome even the greatest of evil. The story highlights the positive effects of being truthful, such as building trust and credibility, and the negative consequence of spreading lies and deceit. By showing the power of honesty and truthfulness, this story provides children with a valuable lesson that will stay with them for a lifetime.

Fun questions about the story:

- What was Jack's mission in the story?
- What was the Shadow Monster's power, and how did Jack defeat it?

Serious questions about the story:

- How do you think Jack's honesty helped her defeat the Shadow Monster?
- In what ways is honesty important in our daily lives, and how can we use it to positively impact the world?

SEVEN

Defeating Morgath: A Young Fairy's Triumph over Evil

*In tonight's story, "The Wonders of Perseverance,"
you'll meet a young fairy named Lily who goes on
a magical adventure to save her kingdom. Along
the way, she learns the importance of never giving
up, no matter how many obstacles she faces.*

❧

ONCE UPON A time, in a magical kingdom filled with colorful creatures and enchanted forests, there lived a young fairy named Marigold. Marigold was 8 years old, with bright eyes and a contagious wide smile. She was brave, curious, and determined, always eager to explore and help others.

"Marigold, come back!" said her mother at the top of her

voice as she flew out of a hole in a large flowerpot. "It's not safe to wander off on your own!"

Marigold ignored her mother's warning and continued on her adventure. As she explored the kingdom, she heard a loud explosion and saw smoke rising. She quickly flew over and saw that the source of the explosion was a wicked witch named Morgath.

Morgath cast a spell to make the kingdom's magic disappear, causing chaos and destruction throughout the land. Marigold knew she had to do something to help.

"Excuse me, can you tell me what happened?" said Marigold to a nearby creature.

"Morgath," said the creature as it slumped away. "She's determined to take over the kingdom and rule with an iron fist. She wants to eliminate all magic from the kingdom and make herself the only source of power."

Marigold's squinted her eyes and fluttered her wings. She needed to be strong to find a way to break the spell and restore the magic to the kingdom.

As she searched for answers, Marigold encountered a wise old owl sitting high in a tree.

"The only way to break the spell," the old owl said, "is to find the three magical crystals hidden in the kingdom."

"Three crystals," Marigold said while she spun around and looked in all directions.

"hoo-h, HOO-hoo-hoo," said the wise old owl.

Marigold was determined to find the crystals and restore the magic to the kingdom, no matter what obstacles came her way. She encountered talking animals, faced dangerous creatures, and braved treacherous landscapes while keeping her determination and bravery strong.

As she approached the witch's castle, Morgath taunted her. "You'll never defeat me, little fairy." The witch cackled as she grabbed her broom. "You don't have what it takes to break the spell."

Marigold replied, "I may be small, but I am determined." She stepped closer to the witch. "I will not give up, no matter what obstacles come my way."

Marigold used her determination and bravery to defeat Morgath in a climactic battle and broke the spell. The magic of the kingdom was restored, and the creatures rejoiced.

Marigold learned the power of perseverance and that with determination and courage, anything is possible. From that day forward, she was known as the bravest fairy in the kingdom and a true inspiration to all who knew her.

"Marigold, you did it!" said her mother as she flew around the flowerpot.

Marigold smiled, "I never gave up, no matter what challenges came my way.

∽

For the reader:

The story, *Defeating Morgath*, demonstrates that perseverance is an important principle to teach children because it encourages them to never give up, even when faced with challenges. When children learn to persist in facing obstacles, they gain the confidence and resilience they need to tackle any problem. This not only helps them succeed in the short term but also prepares them for the ups and downs of life as they grow older. By learning the value of perseverance, children develop a growth mindset and the ability to overcome setbacks and challenges, which will serve them well in their personal and professional lives.

Fun questions about the story:

- What was your favorite part of the story and why?
- If you were Marigold, what would you have done differently and why?

Serious questions about the story:

- How do you think Marigold felt when she faced challenges on her journey to restore the magic to the kingdom?
- Why do you think it is important to persist and not give up, even when faced with difficulties and obstacles?

EIGHT

Defeating Greed: The Adventure of Jack and the Gratitude Treasure

In tonight's story, we will discover the power of gratitude and how appreciating what we have can lead to happiness and satisfaction.

～

ONCE UPON A time, a young boy named Alexander lived in a magical kingdom where creatures and humans lived together in harmony. Alexander was a curious and adventurous child, always eager to explore the world and learn new things. However, he was never content with what he had and always wanted more.

One day, Alexander overheard a group of travelers talking about the "Treasure of Gratitude." The legend, they said, was that it would bring happiness and contentment to whoever possessed it. Intrigued, Alexander decided to set out on a journey to find it.

Along the way, Alexander met a wise old wizard named Merlin.

"Young man, where are you going?" Merlin said as he waved his magical rod over a tiny field mouse.

"I'm searching for the Treasure of Gratitude," Alexander replied. "I've heard that it can bring happiness and contentment."

Merlin smiled. "Gratitude is a powerful thing, young one." The mouse rolled over, squeaked, and ran into the tall grass. "But it is not a physical treasure that can be found and possessed. It is a state of mind that must be cultivated within oneself." Merlin pointed the rod to his head and winked.

Alexander frowned. "What do you mean?"

"Gratitude is about appreciating what you have rather than always wanting more," Merlin said. "It is about recognizing the good in your life and counting your blessings."

The tiny field mouse ran out of the grass, it carried a large acorn in its mouth. It stood on its hind legs in front of Merlin and squeaked several times.

"Keep it, my little friend," Merlin said as he patted the mouse on its head.

Alexander nodded, understanding the wizard's words. He continued on his journey, determined to find the Treasure of Gratitude.

However, Alexander was not the only one searching for the

treasure. The evil sorcerer, Greed, had also heard of it and saw gratitude as a weakness. He believed possessing the treasure would help him achieve his evil plan of ruling the kingdom and enslaving its inhabitants.

As Alexander and Greed drew closer to the treasure, they finally crossed paths.

"Ha! So, you're the one who's been searching for the Treasure of Gratitude!" Greed said with a sneer. "It belongs to me!"

Alexander stood his ground. "I don't think so. Gratitude is a gift to be shared, not something to be possessed by one person."

Greed laughed. "You're a fool, boy. Gratitude is a weakness that I will use to conquer this kingdom."

As the two clashed, Alexander began to understand the true meaning of gratitude. He realized that he had many blessings in his life, and he should be thankful for them. With a newfound appreciation for what he had, Alexander defeated Greed and saved the kingdom.

When he returned home, Alexander shared his newfound understanding of gratitude with everyone he met. He lived the rest of his life counting his blessings and was grateful for all the wonders of life.

⤳

For the reader:

The story, *Defeating Greed*, explores how gratitude is important for children to learn as it helps instill a positive attitude towards life. It promotes contentment with what one has and encourages an appreciation for the good things in life. By emphasizing gratitude, children are taught to look for the good in every situation and to not take things for granted. This leads to a happier and more fulfilling life, as they will be more grateful for the people and experiences they have in their lives. Ultimately, teaching children to be grateful can lead to a more harmonious and grateful society in the future.

Fun questions about the story:

- What did Alexander learn on his journey to find the treasure of gratitude?
- What did Alexander realize about the things he already had in his life that made him happy?

Serious questions about the story:

- What do you think Alexander learned about gratitude during his journey?
- Can you think of something you are grateful for in your life?

NINE

The Battle of the Minds: Mia's Triumph Over the Dark Shadow

In tonight's story, we follow Mia on her journey to find inner peace and learn about the power of mindfulness in her magical kingdom.

ONCE UPON A time, a little girl named Mia lived in a magical kingdom. She was seven years old and had curly brown hair, big brown eyes, and a smile that could light up the world. Mia was curious and kind-hearted but often felt anxious and stressed, as if something was missing in her life. She longed to find inner peace.

One sunny morning, Mia decided to set out on a journey to find the secret to inner peace. She packed a small backpack with food and water and set off into the great unknown.

As Mia walked through the enchanted forest, she met all sorts of talking animals and wise old wizards who shared their knowledge and advice on inner peace.

"Excuse me, Mr. Owl," Mia looked up into the tree. "Do you know the secret to inner peace?"

"Yes, my dear, I do," the owl said as he ruffled his feathers. "Inner peace comes from within, not from external sources." The owl lifted his wing and pointed around the woods. "You must learn to control your thoughts and reactions and not let the outside world affect your inner thoughts. Practice mindfulness, and you will find the strength to face any challenge."

"My inner thoughts," Mia said as she looked at her stomach. "Thank you, wise old owl. But how do I do that?"

"Close your eyes and focus on your breathing." The owl let out a long breath. "Calm your mind and let go of your worries. Remember, your thoughts and emotions are under your control, not the other way around."

Mia took in a deep breath and looked up at the owl with a smile.

"Off with you," the owl said and turned his head around.

Mia continued her journey, determined to find the secret to inner peace. However, she soon realized that she was being pursued by the Dark Shadow, a powerful being who fed on negative energy, like fear and anger. The Dark Shadow was the source of all the stress and anxiety in the kingdom.

"Ha! You will never find inner peace, for it is I who controls the fears and worries of this kingdom," said the Dark Shadow. "Surrender now and I will spare you."

"I won't give up, for I know that inner peace is within me." Mia took in a deep breath and let it out slowly. "I won't let you control my thoughts and emotions."

With her newfound mindfulness and strength, Mia faced the Dark Shadow and challenged him to a battle of the minds. She closed her eyes, took a deep breath, and focused on her breathing. With each inhale and exhale, she felt calmer and more centered.

The Dark Shadow tried to attack Mia with his negative energy, but she remained steadfast, letting go of her worries and fears. With each calm thought, Mia gained more power. In the end, Mia emerged victorious, and the Dark Shadow disappeared, leaving the kingdom in peace.

"I've learned that inner peace comes from within, not external sources." Mia titled her head with a smile. "I can control my thoughts and emotions and find peace in any situation. That's the secret to inner peace."

Mia returned to the kingdom with a peaceful heart and mind, spreading the message of mindfulness and inner peace. She lived happily ever after, knowing that she had the power to find peace within herself, no matter what challenges she faced. And every time she felt anxious or stressed, she would close her eyes, focus on her breathing, and remember the secret to inner peace.

◈

For the reader:

The story, *The Battle of the Minds*, reveals an essential principle for children to learn as it helps them cope with stress and anxiety. Teaching children mindfulness and how to calm their minds can improve their mental health and overall well-being. This lesson helps children understand the importance of managing their mental health and finding ways to positively manage their emotions.

Fun questions about the story:

- Who was Mia's primary opponent on her journey to find inner peace?
- What was the secret Mia learned about finding inner peace?

Serious questions about the story:

- What did you learn about inner peace in the story?
- How do you think you can apply the lessons of mindfulness and inner peace in your own life?

TEN

Embracing Our Differences: A Tale of the Village That Learned to Celebrate Diversity

In tonight's story, "The Beauty of Diversity,"
we will learn about celebrating our differences
and embracing everyone for who they are.

ONCE UPON A time, a little girl named Sarah lived in a small village surrounded by rolling hills and green forests. She lived where everyone looked and acted the same, but Sarah was different. She was curious about the world outside her village and loved daydreaming about far-away lands and the people who lived there.

One day, as Sarah was playing in the meadow near her house, she stumbled upon a group of travelers who were unlike anyone she had ever seen. They had bright, colorful clothes and unique hairstyles and spoke in different languages. Sarah approached them, curious about their backgrounds and cultures.

"Hi there, little one," said a woman with a broad smile and a twinkle in her eye. "Where are you from?"

"I live in the village nearby," Sarah said as she pointed behind her. "Who are you?"

"We are travelers from all over the world," the woman said. "We come together to celebrate our differences and share our cultures."

Sarah was fascinated by the travelers' and couldn't wait to return to her village and share it with everyone. She spent the rest of the day talking to the travelers, learning about their cultures and travels, and making new friends.

When Sarah arrived back in the village, she went straight to Mayor Johnson's house. She wanted to invite the travelers to the village's yearly parade and show everyone the beauty of diversity.

"Mayor Johnson," Sarah said as she knocked on his door. "I have a great idea for the parade this year."

"What is it?" said Mayor Johnson.

"I want to invite the travelers I met today to come and participate in the parade," Sarah said. "They are different from us, but that makes them special. We should celebrate their differences and learn from them."

"I'm afraid I cannot allow that, Sarah," Mayor Johnson said as he shook his head and wrinkled his brow. "Our village is special because we are all the same. We don't need outsiders coming in and disrupting our traditions."

Sarah's lips curled down and her eyes grew sad, but she refused to give up. She returned to the travelers and asked if they would still be willing to participate in the parade, even without the mayor's approval.

"Of course, we will," the woman said. "We believe celebrating our differences is important, and we want to share that message with your village."

On the day of the parade, Sarah and the travelers gathered at the starting line, ready to share their message with the villagers. Mayor Johnson was angry when he saw them, but Sarah stood up to him.

"Everyone is special in their way," Sarah said as she held her head high. "That's what makes the world so beautiful."

The parade began, and the villagers were amazed by the travelers' performances. They sang, danced, and shared their cultures, and the villagers couldn't help but smile and join in.

As the parade ended, the villagers learned a valuable lesson about the beauty of diversity. They no longer saw differences as a threat but as something to be celebrated. From that day forward, the village embraced diversity, accepting everyone for who they were.

And Sarah? She became the village's ambassador of inclusiveness, spreading her message of love and acceptance to all who would listen.

❧

For the reader:

In today's world, it is more important than ever to embrace and celebrate differences among people. The story, *Embracing Our Differences,* promotes inclusiveness and acceptance of others who may be different from us and helps to create a more harmonious and understanding society. Teaching children about the beauty of diversity at a young age helps to instill these values in them. It encourages them to become accepting and empathetic individuals as they grow up.

Fun questions about the story:

- What was your favorite part of the story and why?
- Can you think of a time when you saw someone different from you, and what did you learn from that experience?

Serious questions about the story:

- What is the most important message in the story *Embracing Our Differences?*
- How can we apply the principle of celebrating differences and promoting inclusiveness in our daily lives?

ELEVEN

Timmy and the Evil Sorceress: A Journey of Bravery and Kindness

In tonight's story, we follow Timmy, a young boy with a unique talent for talking to animals, on his journey to save his kingdom from an evil sorceress.

❧

ONCE UPON A time, a young boy named Timmy lived in a magical kingdom filled with rolling hills, lush forests, and colorful villages. Timmy was seven years old, kind, adventurous, and eager to help others. He lived in a small cottage on the edge of the forest with his parents and had a unique talent for talking to animals.

Timmy was playing with his friends in the village square when he overheard two people talking about the evil sorceress who sought to enslave the kingdom. Timmy's heart sank. He couldn't stand the thought of his friends and family under the sorceress's control.

"I have to do something," Timmy thought. "I can't just sit here and watch as the kingdom is destroyed."

So, Timmy set out on a journey to stop the sorceress and save the kingdom, determined to stand up for what was right.

Timmy encountered many obstacles as he traveled through the dangerous forests and crossed treacherous rivers. But he never gave up. He always found a way to overcome challenges, using his bravery and kindness to help those in need.

"Excuse me, young traveler," said an old grey horse next to a stream. "Why do you travel alone?"

"I am on a mission to stop the evil sorceress and save the kingdom," Timmy said. "I can't sit by and do nothing while she enslaves my friends and family."

The grey horse nodded. "Your bravery and kindness are commendable, Timmy." The grey horse turned its head left and then right. "But the sorceress is a powerful foe, and you must be careful. She has many minions and tricks up her sleeve."

Timmy thanked the grey horse for his advice and continued on his journey. He met other creatures of the forest who joined him on his quest, each drawn to his bravery and kindness.

When Timmy finally reached the sorceress's castle, he was met by a group of her minions.

"Who are you, and why are you here?" said the most oversized minion with narrow eyes.

Timmy stepped forward, bravery shining in his eyes. "I am Timmy, and I'm here to stop the sorceress. I won't let her enslave the kingdom. I will stand up for what is right and fight for those who can't fight for themselves."

The minions laughed. "You're just a small boy. You have no chance against our mistress."

But Timmy refused to back down. He summoned all his bravery and fought with all his might, using his kindness and wit to defeat the sorceress's minions one by one.

Finally, it was time for the final confrontation. The sorceress taunted Timmy, trying to intimidate him with her magic, but Timmy stood his ground.

"I won't let you hurt my friends and family," Timmy said. "I will stand up for what is right and fight for those who cannot fight for themselves."

The sorceress laughed. "You are just a small boy, Timmy. You have no chance against me."

But Timmy proved her wrong. He used courage and kindness to defeat the sorceress and save the kingdom.

In the end, Timmy returned home to his cottage, hailed as a hero by the kingdom's people. They celebrated his bravery and kindness, and Timmy realized he had learned a valuable lesson. He had discovered the power of courage and kindness to overcome evil and that no matter how small or powerless one may seem, one can make a difference in the world.

෴

For the reader:

The story, *Timmy and the Evil Sorceress,* teaches a valuable life lesson to children. Through Timmy's journey, children can learn the importance of standing up for what is right, helping others, and the power of bravery and kindness. It demonstrates that no matter how small or powerless one may seem, one can make a difference in the world and overcome adversity. The story is an excellent way to instill positive values in children and inspire them to be their best versions. It helps to build their self-esteem and reinforces the idea that everyone can make a positive impact in their unique way.

Fun questions about the story:

- Who is Timmy's best animal friend?
- What is the name of the evil sorceress who wants to take over the kingdom?

Serious questions about the story:

- Why was it important for Timmy to stand up for what was right?
- How did Timmy's actions help others in the kingdom?

TWELVE

A Home for the Little Bird: The Story of the Giving Tree

In tonight's story, we will follow the adventures of the Giving Tree, who lives in a magical forest filled with talking trees and animals.

❧

ONCE UPON A time, in a magical forest filled with talking trees and animals, there lived a Giving Tree. It was a kind and selfless tree, always eager to help those in need. The Giving Tree was the heart and soul of the forest, loved by all who knew it.

One day, a young rabbit hopped up to the Giving Tree and asked, "Dear Giving Tree, can you give me some shade?"

The Giving Tree bent its branches and shaded the rabbit

with its leaves. The rabbit sat in the cool, comfortable spot and looked up at the Giving Tree, "Thank you so much! You are so kind."

Over time, more and more animals came to the Giving Tree for help. They asked for leaves for their nests, apples to eat, and even wood to build their homes. And the Giving Tree never hesitated to give, even as it began to run out of resources.

But one day, the Giving Tree was feeling tired. It looked up at the sky and whispered, "I have given so much, but what will happen to me when I have nothing left to give?"

Just then, a little bird landed on one of its branches and chirped, "Dear Giving Tree, may I have a twig to build my nest?"

The Giving Tree thought for a moment. "I'm sorry, little bird. I don't have any twigs left to give you."

The bird looked sad and flew away. The Giving Tree felt terrible, and its branch fell limp. "Maybe I could have done something else to help the bird."

Suddenly, the bird returned. "I had an idea. Instead of a twig, could I have your trunk to build my home?"

The Giving Tree was surprised but happy to help. "Of course! You can take my trunk and make it into a home. That way, you will always have a place to stay."

The bird thanked the Giving Tree and flew away with its new home. From that day on, the Giving Tree was no longer just a tree. It became a home, a source of love and comfort, and a symbol of selflessness and generosity.

Every day, the animals in the magical forest would visit and sing songs of thanks to the Giving Tree. They would sing,

"Dear Giving Tree, you are our friend,

You never hesitate to lend,

Your leaves, your shade, your trunk too,

A symbol of love, forever true."

And the Giving Tree would smile and feel the joy of generosity.

ᣟ

For the reader:

This story, *A Home for the Little Bird*, teaches the value of generosity and selflessness. The Giving Tree is a positive role model, demonstrating the joy and fulfillment that can come from helping others, even when it means sacrificing one's resources. By showing the impact that one selfless act can have on others and one's own life, the story encourages children to be kind and to think of others before themselves. The story also has a clear and straightforward message that is easy for children to understand and apply in their lives.

Fun questions about the story:

- What did the Giving Tree give to the boy as he grew older?
- What did the Giving Tree wish for at the end of the story?

Serious questions about the story:

- Why do you think the Giving Tree was so eager to help everyone in the forest?
- What do you think you can do to show generosity and selflessness to others, just like the Giving Tree did?

THIRTEEN

Lily and Gorg: Heroes of the Forest

*In tonight's story, we follow the adventures
of a young girl named Mary who sets out to
find a stolen key in a magical forest.*

⤜

O NCE UPON A time, a young girl named Mary lived in a small village surrounded by a dense forest filled with magical creatures. Mary was seven years old and had an adventurous spirit. She loved exploring the forest and discovering new things.

One day, Mary heard a rumor that the key to unlocking a powerful magical object had been stolen from the village. She was determined to find the key and bring it back so that the object could be used for the good of the community.

She asked around the village, but no one knew anything

about the key. So, she decided to venture into the forest to look for it herself.

As she explored, she stumbled upon a mischievous and cunning creature named Gorg. Gorg had the key in his possession and was determined to keep it himself.

Mary walked up to Gorg and looked him in the eyes. "Would give please give me the key?"

Gorg stepped forward and stared at Mary. "Why should I give it to you?" Gorg said with a sneer.

"The key doesn't belong to you," Mary said. "It belongs to the village and should be used for the good of everyone."

Gorg laughed. "You're too young to understand. I'll never give it to you."

Mary was determined to get the key back but didn't want to take it by force. That wouldn't be responsible or honest.

So, she walked back to the village and thought about the situation. She realized that she needed to devise a plan to get the key back without breaking the principles of responsibility and honesty.

The next day, Mary returned to the forest and approached Gorg with a proposition. "I understand why you want to keep the key," she said. "But wouldn't it be better if we worked together to use it for the good of the village?"

Gorg was skeptical at first, but he eventually agreed to work with Mary. Together, they retrieved the key and returned to the village, where they unlocked the magical object and used it for the entire community's benefit.

The villagers were amazed and grateful. Mary and Gorg

had shown them the value of responsibility and honesty. And from that day on, they were known as heroes in the village.

Years went by, and Mary and Gorg continued to work together to make the world a better place. They explored the forest and helped the village whenever they could. Their story was passed down from generation to generation, inspiring others to be responsible and honest.

One day, as they were walking through the forest, Gorg turned to Mary and said, "Do you remember when we first met, and you asked me for the key?"

"Of course, I do," Mary said with a smile. "That was the day we became friends."

Gorg nodded. "And it was the day we showed the villagers the value of responsibility and honesty."

"Yes, it was." Mary nodded. "And it's a lesson that will always be with us."

And, from that day on, Mary and Gorg continued to walk through the forest, using their responsibility and honesty to make the world a better place.

∽

For the reader:

The story, *Lily and Gorg*, explores the values of responsibility and honesty through the character of Mary. The story shows that these values are essential in personal relationships and contributing to the greater good of a community. The story also emphasizes the importance of collaboration and working together to achieve a common goal, which is a valuable lesson for children to learn.

Fun questions about the story:

- What kind of creature was Gorg?
- What did Lily use to get the key back?

Serious questions about the story:

- Why was it necessary for Lily to be responsible and honest in the story?
- What could have happened if Lily wasn't responsible and honest?

FOURTEEN

The Hardworking Ant: A Tale of Perseverance and Determination

In tonight's story, we follow the journey of a hardworking ant named Anto as he tries to gather food for the winter.

✌

ONCE UPON A time, a hardworking ant named Anto lived in a magical forest filled with talking animals and whimsical creatures. Anto lived in a colony in the heart of the forest and was always the first one to volunteer for any task that needed to be done.

One day, the colony's leader, the wise old ant with one bent antenna, asked Anto to gather food for the winter. Anto eagerly accepted the challenge and set out to gather as much food as he could.

As Anto was collecting acorns, he came across a buzzing bee. The bee, named Buzz, was lazily lounging on a flower.

"Hey there, Anto!" Buzz said in a happy high, pitched voice. "What are you up to?"

"I'm gathering food for the winter," Anto said and continued to collect acorns.

Buzz scoffed. "Why bother? Winter will be over soon enough." Buzz zipped around Anto. "You should take a break and come enjoy the sun with me."

Anto shook his head. "I want to make sure my colony has enough food to last the winter. I'm determined to do my best."

Buzz laughed. "Your determination is admirable, but it's a waste of time." Buzz landed on a flower and crossed his two front legs. "Trust me, you won't even notice winter passing by if you relax and have some fun."

But Anto wasn't swayed. He continued to work, gathering more and more food for his colony. Buzz continued to distract him, but Anto refused to be deterred from his task.

Days passed, and Anto's pile of food grew larger and larger. He was working harder than ever, and his determination never wavered.

When winter finally arrived, Anto presented his colony with a huge pile of food. The colony was overjoyed, and Anto was praised for his hard work and perseverance.

"See, I told you it was a waste of time," Buzz said in a grumbly voice as he watched Anto being celebrated. "I could have been enjoying the sun this whole time instead of gathering food."

Anto smiled at Buzz. "It may have been hard work, but the reward of ensuring my colony is taken care of is worth it. The rewards of hard work and perseverance are always worth it in the end."

Buzz nodded, understanding the importance of hard work and determination. From that day forward, he changed his lazy ways and learned the importance of working hard and never giving up.

And Anto, the patient ant, was remembered as a shining example of the rewards of hard work and perseverance. His story inspired all the creatures in the forest to work hard and never give up on their goals.

⤚

For the reader:

The story, *The Hardworking Ant*, is important because it teaches children the principle of the rewards of hard work and perseverance. It demonstrates that putting in effort and sticking to a task can lead to success, even when faced with distractions and temptations to give up. The story provides a positive example for children to follow, inspiring them to work hard and never give up on their goals, showing them the potential benefits of determination and persistence.

Fun questions about the story:

- Who was your favorite character in the story, and why?
- Can you imagine a time when you had to work hard to achieve something?

Serious questions about the story:

- What do you think Anto learned from his experience in the story?
- Why do you think it is important to be patient and persevere, even when things get tough?

FIFTEEN

Luna's Emotional Adventure

In tonight's story, "The Rainbow of Emotions," we follow the adventures of Luna the unicorn as she learns about emotions and how to manage them.

❦

ONCE UPON A time, a young unicorn named Luna lived in a magical land filled with colorful creatures like unicorns and fairies. Luna was curious, adventurous, and loved to explore. However, she also struggled with her emotions and found it difficult to understand and manage them.

One day, as Luna was wandering through the enchanted forest, she encountered a mischievous and cruel fairy named Shadow. Shadow loved to play pranks on the creatures of the magical land, causing them to feel all sorts of emotions.

"Hello there, Luna," said Shadow with a sly grin. "What's wrong? You seem upset."

Luna sighed and looked down at the ground. "I'm just

feeling so many emotions right now." She let out a huff. "I don't know what to do with them."

Shadow chuckled and said, "Well, why don't you come with me? I have a surprise that will make you feel even more emotions."

Luna was hesitant, but her curiosity got the better of her and she followed Shadow deep into the forest. Shadow led her to a clearing where he had caused chaos and trouble, making all the creatures of the magical land feel upset, angry, and frustrated.

Shadow cackled with delight, "Ha! Look at them all! They're so upset, just like you!"

Luna felt her emotions rise, but she refused to let Shadow control her. She closed her eyes and took a deep breath, trying to calm herself down.

"What are you doing?" asked Shadow, confused.

Luna opened her eyes and replied, "I'm learning to understand and manage my emotions. I don't want to let you or anyone else control my feelings."

Shadow was taken aback, but he wasn't about to give up that easily. He continued to play pranks and cause trouble, trying to make Luna feel sad, angry, and frustrated. But each time, Luna used her emotional intelligence to recognize and control her feelings.

"You're getting better at this," said Shadow with a sneer. "But I can still make you feel angry."

Luna was determined. She focused on her breathing and

thought about happy memories. Suddenly, she felt a smile spread across her face.

"You're not making me feel angry," said Luna with a grin. "I'm in control of my emotions."

As Luna continued on her journey, she encountered other creatures who also struggled with their emotions. She helped them understand and manage their feelings, just as she was learning to do for herself.

With each new challenge, Luna grew stronger and more confident. Eventually, she was ready to face Shadow once and for all.

The two clashed in a magical battle, with Shadow trying to make Luna feel all sorts of emotions and Luna using her emotional intelligence to remain calm and focused. In the end, Luna defeated Shadow and brought peace back to the magical land.

From that day on, Luna was known as the protector of emotional intelligence. She traveled the land, helping creatures understand and manage their emotions and bringing joy and peace wherever she went.

And so, the importance of emotional intelligence was passed down from generation to generation, becoming a timeless lesson in the magical land.

❧

For the reader:

This story teaches children the importance of understanding and managing emotions, a crucial life skill. It demonstrates how important it is to understand and manage one's emotions and shows that anyone can develop these skills with practice. The story also highlights the consequences of allowing emotions to control us and the power we have to control our emotions and bring peace and joy to ourselves and those around us. Through the character of Luna, the story encourages children to be brave and take control of their emotions, inspiring them to develop their emotional intelligence.

Fun questions about the story:

- What were some of the different emotions Luna felt throughout the story?
- Can you act out how Shadow tried to upset Luna?

Serious questions about the story:

- How did Luna learn to control her emotions?
- What can you do when you feel overwhelmed by your emotions?

ABOUT THE AUTHOR

Jennifer Middleton is a young mother of two who is passionate about storytelling. She is inspired by her childhood memories of her father weaving magical tales for her and her siblings at bedtime. With a keen eye for detail and a vivid imagination, Jennifer has created a collection of stories that not only entertain children, but also educate and inspire them. Her stories are set in today's society and are designed to spark the imaginations of 4 to 8-year-olds, with a touch of fantasy and whimsy. Jennifer's goal is to provide children with an enjoyable and educational experience through her stories, which are filled with important lessons about bravery, kindness, and determination. Her own children are her biggest fans, and she hopes that her stories will be enjoyed by families for generations to come.